MOUNT TERROR

E.L. GILES

Available from Black Hare Press

SHORT READS

WARDENCLYFFE by GREGG CUNNINGHAM
HADES 11 by PAUL WARMERDAM
BLOOD AND SILK by ZOEY XOLTON
AS ABOVE, SO BENEATH by JOSHUA D. TAYLOR
THE RISE OF THE GREAT OLD ONE by JASMINE
JARVIS
DEAD MAN WALKING by DAVID GREEN
CHRYSALIS by KIMBERLY REI
MOUNT TERROR by E.L. GILES
HELL HATH NO FURY by CHISTO HEALY
THE RECKONING by STEPHANIE SCISSOM

UNDERGROUND

MIRACLE GROWTH by TIM MENDEES
THE RETURN by GABRIELLA BALCOM
UNDERGROUND by STEVEN STREETER
WHISPERS IN THE DARK by K.B. ELIJAH
SWIRLING DARKNESS by SAM M. PHILLIPS
THE GATE TO THE UNDERWORLD by E.L. GILES
COLD AS HELL by NEEN COHEN
THOSE OF THE LIGHT by NICOLA CURRIE
TIME'S ABYSS by JAMES PYLES
UNDERWORLD GAMES by JONATHAN D. STIFFY
PLACE OF CAVES by CHARLOTTE O'FARRELL
AFTER THE FALL by STEPHEN HERCZEG
BEYOND HUMAN by MATHEW CLARKE
THE FALL OF PACIFICA by M. SYDNOR JR.

For the pneumonia that kept my girlfriend bedded and allowed me to finish this story (kidding. I love you, babe.)

E.L. Giles, January 2021

TABLE OF CONTENTS

CHAPTER I

This is Captain Ernst Land. Do you copy? The Dawn is sinking. I repeat: our ship is sinking. We are trapped on Ross Island... Conditions have become impossible... We were coming back from the Markham Plateau...took us all unaware... McMurdo Sound's base camp destroyed... Expect to lose communication in a moment. Can't seem to find refuge... Prisoner of this desert of ice and madness... It was a mistake. Oh, my God! I shouldn't have come here... We've unearthed...something...terrible... I realise my mistake. If you are receiving this message, do not come here. For God's sake, do not come here to rescue us... We are already doomed... We are...

Cold sweat gathered over my face as I read through the entire transcription of Land's last transmission. I must have read it a hundred times already, yet nothing about it made sense to me. A shiver crawled up my spine, and I gripped tightly at my glass of scotch, barely aware of the growing numbness in my hand. I emptied the contents of the glass in one gulp, hoping it would bring me some peace during these troubling hours. This escapism proved futile, as I realised the ghost of dread still inhabited my mind, permeating it with an icy horror

I couldn't lift from my soul. I raised my eyes from the crumpled piece of paper and started walking to and fro in my cabin. The old wooden floor creaked noisily, swaying softly under my feet and disturbing for a moment my dark train of thought.

What happened to you, old fool? I wondered. I concentrated again on the words laid out on the thick, pulpy paper, more precisely on the silent spots in the disconnected message that had us all baffled. The words as they appeared on the paper didn't do justice to the grim tone of Land's transmission that had leaked out into the communication room, affecting everyone. The ink couldn't speak, nor could it imitate Land's frightened voice. The dots connecting the message could not reproduce the ominous hissing static that had muted Land throughout his message, as if something was aware of the danger his words might represent.

At exactly five in the morning, I walked out of my cabin and began inspecting one last time every corner of the *Ulysses*, a converted schooner-rigged steamship of the same kind Shackleton had sailed with during his 1921 expedition. The *Ulysses* had been refitted for the harsh conditions one could expect from the untamed waters surrounding an aeon-dead continent. There, along the coastline of Antarctica, we would set up our camp and start our research, and we wouldn't come back to New Zealand before this whole mystery was unravelled.

What could possibly go wrong? I thought, staring intently across the placid sea. We had dogs, sleds, skis, and food in sufficient quantity. We had also been provided with portable wireless transmitters and transmission rigs of the latest model, which had specifically been designed for military use. We had a crew of the boldest kind, most of them experienced with the Antarctic climate. Some of them had sailed with Shackleton or had taken part in the investigation of the tragedy that had struck Scott and the Terra Nova Expedition so many years ago. Was that what we were going to investigate now? A tragedy? Was there a chance they had survived?

I shook my head. The man I used to know wouldn't have given up. No! Land was the fiercest explorer I had ever known. Overly eccentric, but without a doubt a survivor. Still, it had been difficult to recognise the man who had spoken that message. It was the voice of a broken man, one who had fallen into the grip of inexplicable terror.

It hadn't taken long for the rumours to spread throughout the world. The popular belief was that Land hadn't been cut out for such a difficult expedition—a belief greatly influenced by the papers, which didn't miss a chance to relate his peculiar love of occult books and the supernatural.

The gossip even went so far as to speculate that the extreme climate and loneliness of the Antarctic had overcome his reason and sanity. But none of them heard what I heard, and none of them knew Land as I knew him—which must explain why they wanted me to lead this expedition. I believed he had experienced something truly terrible. And I didn't doubt Land's sanity had been shaken and perhaps shattered by something—something he had discovered, *unearthed*. And he was trying to warn us.

"Do you think they're still alive?" asked First Officer Thomas Lashly, a senior seaman whose athletic build, intelligence, and eloquence of speech clashed greatly with his caveman features—long hair, a thick black beard and untrimmed brows, and skin so thick it seemed that only diamonds could scratch its surface. He came closer and, realising he had my attention, resumed speaking, "It's very unlikely that they survived so long in such a place, don't you think?"

I sighed. "Land's a survivor of the most peculiar kind. Trust me, he has seen many of the most extreme places. If anyone could do it, it's Land."

"Sorry, I forgot you knew him." Thomas smiled at me, but it didn't quite reach his eyes. Something was bothering him. "But surviving the Antarctic winter is a whole other world. Eight months have passed. Their camp was destroyed by the storm. They have no ship anymore. What would they have done? How would have they survived? What would they have eaten? Penguins? Pardon me, but it just seems unlikely that…well, you know…"

I placed a hand on Thomas's broad shoulder and squeezed it gently. I said nothing. I was far too aware of such things, but still, I allowed myself some hope.

It took a long moment before Thomas dared expose his apprehensions to me again. "What do you think happened there? What did they unear—"

"I don't know, Thomas," I said, releasing a weary sigh. I had been haunted by far too many dreams since hearing that transmission. The question tormented my mind restlessly: what did they unearth? What had Land's motivation behind this trip been?

All kinds of theories had formed in my mind, fuelled by the most horrendous monsters and abominations found in Land's book collection— one book in particular, an untitled antique. One whose grotesque appearance utterly disgusted me. One whose origin had remained a mystery. Land had often shown it to me, but had never let me inspect it to satisfy my curiosity. He had frequently recited from the book many obscure excerpts about an intelligent race, predating the first *Homo sapiens* and living in the subterranean of unknown regions, worshipping deities no human had ever heard about. Land had, in fact, based his early research on this book; research that had ultimately digressed into utter mysticism and cosmic fantasy rather than putting forth actual scientific evidence, which had annoyed many of his peers and earned him the nickname *Bouffon*.

"You look tired, Henry. Are you sure you're all right?"

"I'm just fine, Thomas. Don't worry about me."

I stared into space as the sun rose slowly, emblazing the horizon with a palette of vivid orange, violet, and pink colours, spreading this canvas over the placid waters surrounding Oamaru. And here we sat aboard the *Ulysses*, which shone with the most iridescent hues of golden brown and yellow. Its pillar-like masts stretched sky-high like statues of Titans, overhanging the world in anticipation of Poseidon's wrath.

Thomas brought his pipe to his lips, filled it with some tobacco, and lit it. He puffed out and then handed it to me. I inhaled deeply, filling my lungs with the soothing smoke. The first jolts gently shook the ship's hull as we left the tranquillity of the coastal waters of New Zealand.

What could possibly go wrong?

CHAPTER II

December 15, 1935

Since we left the calm Pacific waters and crossed the unwelcoming barrier into the Austral Sea, the winds have switched and grown in hellish proportion. For a few days now, a dark and ominous veil has covered the southern sky, and not once has the sun pierced through the thick, amorphous clouds. It's like the entire world has suddenly been plunged into an eternal twilight. Tides, sometimes as high as fifteen feet, pound mercilessly and restlessly on the ship, stronger, it seems, than a hundred iron hammers striking against an anvil. As a result of these chaotic conditions, one of the engines has been severely damaged and needs temporary repair, but we don't have the materials necessary to fix it. Also, on the night of December 12, we lost two seamen: Chapman and Taylor, who both fell overboard into the icy, black waters after a particularly monstrous series of destructive waves hit the Ulysses. Never in my whole life have I witnessed such fury from Nature. Never have I felt this insignificant, this powerless and lost. It was like the very sea rejected us, refused our presence here in this region, like some higher forces have decided to protect it at any cost. Damn, I sound like Land! More strangely, I think I understand what he meant when he said that we are nothing after all. Just simple, primitive machines surrounded by forces we cannot in any way control.

As I am now writing these lines and putting everything into perspective, I've come to the conclusion that there are two options I must consider. The idea of turning back has been rolling around in the back of my mind for a while now. But there is also a morbid curiosity that has taken a grip on me and a need to understand what happened to Land. What did they unearth? What happened to them to cause such strain and terror in his voice? I have never known him to be that afraid of anything. No matter how hard I try to forget them, Land's last words still haunt me every second, every minute...more and more now that we are approaching the Ross Archipelago and McMurdo Sound.

I closed my diary, securely locked it in my drawer, and then walked towards the door of my cabin after giving a quick, furtive glance towards my cot. Still, it appeared uninviting to me. The need to sleep or chase after respite of any sort felt so distant that I'd given up on trying to find slumber. Not even scotch-induced naps worked, as my brain constantly laboured to keep the worries alive. How many sleepless days had tormented my strained soul? How many miles of unfathomable abysses had we really crossed through?

Passing the door, I forced myself not to look at the table on which the map was spread, its corners clamped to the thick wooden top, and the compass and the pen lying where I'd left them. Exhaustion had hindered me from working out our position.

A particularly insidious wave hit the hull just as I reached the first mast, sending a tremor across the ship from bow to stern. I gripped at the cables on the mast and waited for the ship to stabilise somewhat before continuing. I then used the handrails and made my way up to the bow, where I positioned myself to search the horizon with my telescope.

"Still nothing in sight?" shouted Thomas as he reached my side. I shook my head without putting my scope down. "Are we los—"

"We're right on course," I said, trying to hide my own uncertainty about the matter. "We are following precisely the route we are supposed to."

Thomas stayed beside me, and his presence grew into a source of stress. I already knew of most of his apprehensions, since I shared them. I knew that the rations were rapidly being depleted. The dogs were beginning to act strangely, like they were going mad or simply becoming bored and getting excited and overly aggressive. I had noticed, too, that the mood among the crew had reached its bleakest state yet. And as much as I gazed about the horizon, I couldn't seem to find an end to this raging sea—no calm whatsoever. Worse, I had not even been able to decipher with my instruments the distance separating us from the bloody continent.

I had just closed my eyes for a moment, to gather my wits, when Thomas yelled, shaking my shoulder excitedly.

"Look at that!"

I snapped my eyes open and was filled with a warming hope that we would finally see the outline of snowy mountains and the icy shore of Antarctica. But the sight of lightning bolts illuminating the titanic clouds and the rumbling of thunder deflated me.

"What the hell?" I murmured, staring at the clouds that were darkening into a fathomless blackness. The wind unexpectedly switched, now blowing from the west, hurtling the ship sideways. The shaken frigate swayed and leaned at a dangerous angle towards the water. The hull creaked and tremored like it was about to be torn in half, and I heard the cries of a man as he fell into the water. A second burst of wind damaged the first mast and broke a cable, which snapped inches from my head. Startled, my hands slipped from the rail— if it hadn't been for Thomas, who caught me just in time, I would have fallen overboard too.

"Thanks," I said, faltering. My heart pummelled in my chest like it might break the ribs, caging it. I gripped the handrail with two hands now, my head lowered to protect myself from the icy shards of rain. That was it. I was done with this voyage. "We're going—"

A thunderclap bellowed through the raging sky, deafening. It illuminated the abysmal darkness temporarily with its violet light, outlining the morphing shapes of the monstrous stratus, which seemed to have gathered into a single entity over us, readying itself to inflict its most powerful bolt upon us.

"That's impossible..." said Thomas, who seemed on the brink of panic. A thunderstorm erupting in the coldest place on Earth, this desert? It was simply impossible, inexplicable, yet it was happening before my eyes. Suddenly, the black veil of twilight was lifted, as if to welcome new actors onto the stage. Before my horrified eyes appeared the silhouette of the dead volcanoes surrounding McMurdo Sound, elevated over the desolate Antarctic Plateau.

I scratched my head, confused. We had reached our destination, and against all odds, survived the tempestuous sea and merciless winds. But the sensation remained that we should turn back, for the demonic weather tarried overhead, swirling around as if waiting for us to land before trapping us in its deadly tentacles.

Gradually, the storm clouds evaporated and disappeared, sucked into the peak of Mount Terror, as if the mountain itself was the source of the calamity that had plagued us since we entered the Austral Sea. I studied the manifestation, a blend of awe and terror fighting inside of me as I tried to assure myself that everything happening had a scientific explanation. But I found none.

The sky cleared to a paler shade of grey, less ominous, and with one last rumble, the thunder died, but not without whipping through the sky one last time, bathing the immediate world in an apocalyptical blood-red hue. The piping wind abruptly died down to a manageable though glacial breeze, much colder than what I would have expected for summer in the Antarctic. The land fully appeared now before us, its ethereal white snow dully reflecting the mournful tapestry.

Thomas stared at me, his eyes round with fright. He then looked over my shoulder at the team of three men trying to rescue the poor boy who had likely already succumbed to the murky waters. He sighed noisily.

"Do you think it's safe to drop anchor?" he asked. "I mean, may I suggest that we sit for a moment and assess the whole situation? We don't even know what happened just now. And what if another storm like that hits us and sinks our ship, just like Land's—"

"I know," I said. I leaned against the handrail, temporarily weakened by the weight of my duty towards the men I had led here. My head felt heavy on my shoulders, yet light and dizzy with adrenaline. "But we've made it here. And I think it wouldn't be taken well by the investors who funded the voyage if we just turned around and left without at least trying to find Land and retrieve all the information and materials we could, don't you think? Keep in mind, this rescue trip is more political than anything else. Sorry, but that's the way it is."

Thomas dropped his head and rested his chin against his chest. For a moment, he looked like a pitiful dog, and I did feel a certain amount of compassion for him.

"You're probably right," he mumbled, and raising his head, forced a smile and nodded.

"Good, then."

CHAPTER III

January 02, 1936

I couldn't quite describe even if I truly wanted the scene that welcomed us when we landed and located the site where Land had erected his camp— for no camp exists anymore, only debris scattered around a 2-kilometre radius. No words exist that would do justice to the sight of utter destruction and horror.

As I said, Land's base camp was completely ravaged, just like he said in his last transmission. What we didn't know, though, was that at least half of the members of his expedition were decimated along with it. The bodies we have unearthed were all frozen in the most horrible positions, their hands drawn up in a futile attempt at protection. The thing that struck me most was the sheer fright in their eyes. How could this have been caused by a storm?

After we buried the bodies and took stock of the situation, we decided to set up our camp near the vestiges of Land's so we could investigate the terrain more easily. The portable relay antenna and main communication devices have all been installed in and around my own tent, for I am the most experienced with such apparatuses. It took us all a few days to leave the memory of the terrible voyage and the sight of Land's camp behind us. Though the mood remains quite dark and the dogs sometimes seem to acquire curious and sudden fits of rage, as if able to sense something we can't, everyone works with a restless obstinacy to unearth every piece of paper, every scrap of information, and all the equipment that was buried in the snow. It's strange that sometimes only the most awful and gruesome things have the power to ignite our motivation and push us to work our hardest. I feel in every man a desire to do justice to Land's memory, as well as his work here, and to try everything possible to find the man, alive or not. So far, nothing that we have found has allowed us to reconstruct the events preceding Land's transmission. We have not even located a single piece of the Dawn, though we haven't yet covered a quarter of the entire area, nor have we explored the mountains, which my gut screams at me have something to do with Land's disappearance.

Three days ago I sent a team equipped with portable communication rigs, sledges, and dogs to walk the Markham Plateau, which was where Land was supposedly coming back from when the storm hit them. The team is being led by Jarvis Alpert, who participated in Scott's rescue mission. I must admit...

"The sledges are ready," said Thomas, who had entered the tent without me noticing it. I dropped my pen and closed my diary. I then put it beside me on the wobbly table that I had hastily constructed from scrap and debris I'd found onsite. "The dogs are surprisingly calm today. I hope nothing will trigger them."

"Perfect, perfect," I said without much enthusiasm. Thomas frowned at me. I got up from my cot and walked across the tent, then picked up a heavy metal box that was padded on all sides with absorbent material and handed it to Thomas. "Your portable radio. There are enough batteries and vacuum tubes to operate it for hours. You know how it works, right?"

Thomas nodded, but I instructed him regardless about the general use and functionality of the transmitter, explaining how its signal would be caught by the antenna and then transmitted through my own receiver. I then sketched for him as simply as I could the main circuitry, telling him how to avoid trouble and how to make repairs. I was aware that Thomas already knew it all, but I nonetheless went on with my explanations, preferring to busy myself and my brain rather than ruminate over my current apprehensions. I put my hand in my pocket and felt the crumpled paper that had never left it. Land's last message.

"You know you can't avoid sleep eternally, right?" Thomas said, for he knew all too well what I had been up to the last few nights. Reading the transcription. Waiting by the radio for Alpert to call me with his latest update. I had not heard from him for two days ago, which was worrying. "I'm pretty sure they're all right. Alpert's a big boy, and he's participated in I don't know how many rescue missions already. It's probably just that his radio is dead, and he doesn't know how to repair it."

"You may be right," I said, forcing a smile. It was true that Alpert wasn't particularly competent with technology. The nearly sixty-year-old man would have preferred a good old smoke signal over using the radio, if I may say so.

"Don't worry," Thomas went on, smiling, though it didn't reach his face. He, too, had his own demons at the moment, I supposed. I would have given anything to drop all of my current tasks and go exploring with them. "We'll just circumnavigate Ross Island and search for any signs of Land or wreckage from the *Dawn*. And if the weather starts to worsen, we'll let you know. And if we can't call you for some reason and we're in trouble, I'll fire three times, just like you told Alpert."

I nodded, and Thomas left my tent. As I watched him and his team leave camp, thoughts of Alpert haunted my mind. What could have possibly gone so wrong that Alpert would stop checking in with me? The weather had been fair for many days now. If they'd found anything relevant to Land's tragedy, he should have called me immediately. If they had run into trouble, I surely would have heard the crackling noise of a gunshot piercing the air. We would have come to their rescue. *No gunshots, no problem,* I tried to tell myself. But why wouldn't he answer my calls?

Once every hour, my exhausted voice filled the tent. "Chapelton to Alpert. Chapelton to Alpert. Do you copy? I repeat. Do you copy?"

But the only answer was a sinister crackling noise and a low hum, underneath which a constant white noise lived and nothing else. I turned to the desk where we'd laid each of the pieces of paper we had gathered from the site. I stared at them—disconnected pieces of an impossible puzzle—and despite my best efforts to match them together and comprehend what they conveyed, nothing worked until the words "sporadic seismic waves" popped out to me. I read the many journal entries over and over again, trying to find any correlating evidence. Was it one of the many dormant volcanoes slowly rising back to life? Was it another strange manifestation that no human, even as intelligent as Land was, could explain? Did this seismic wave have a connection with Land's strange claim that they had unearthed something? So many questions, so few answers. Chaotic thoughts began to swim in my exhausted mind as I tried to find any logic behind it all.

It was about midnight when I finally decided to give up on my task and go to bed. But then I heard it: the sinister howling of a dog! At first, there only seemed to be one dog, but then another one joined in the cacophony, and then two more. They began to chant in unison their macabre symphony.

I jumped out of my cot and ran outside of my tent, armed with my old, trusty six-shot revolver. The pallid nocturnal sun shone dully, wrapped inside its constant cover of lead-grey clouds and illuminating a scene I wasn't prepared to face. Near a dozen dogs with white, bristled fur like rabid wolves stood snarling, their lips curled, displaying prominent incisors. I recognised almost all of them as Alpert's own sledge dogs, as they bore red collars around their necks. Two or three of them I had never seen before, and I would have preferred to avoid seeing their blood-smeared fur and demonic eyes. I aimed my pistol towards the closest of the animals. The dog barked twice, and the horrible chorus stopped suddenly.

"What the hell is going on?" I heard someone say behind me. "Let's shoot them all dead."

"Wait," I advised. "Don't do anything stupid. We need to understand what's going on with them."

The very air surrounding us grew thick with stark fear, heavy and bone chilling. For what seemed to me an eternity, the dogs stared at us in a baffling silence, and we responded in kind. Then came a debilitated whining, transported by a sudden lifted breeze. At first, it wasn't anything decipherable, as the wind did have a tendency to play tricks. But then the whining took on human characteristics, like the pathetic noises a patient in a madhouse might utter. A shape, limping forward slowly, entered my line of vision. I squinted my eyes, framing the silhouette of the newcomer, and ignored the dogs surrounding us.

"He...lp..." came the voice, faint but understandable, recognisable.

"Alpert! It's Alpert!" I exclaimed, shocked.

I tried to move towards him, but the nearest dog snarled at me, and I stopped.

"Alpert!" I called, but he didn't seem to see us. He kept on calling for help, his head bowed and his back rounded like he was about to fall facedown onto the ground. "Alpert, we're right here."

Alpert finally raised his head, and our eyes met. I almost dropped my revolver at the sight—black, tenebrous holes devoid of eyeballs.

"Alpert, follow my voice!" I cried. "Follow my voice. We'll take care of you."

"What about the dogs?" asked a seaman who was nicknamed Comanche—a tall, bulky native from North America who feared nothing and no one. But even Comanche's voice held a certain amount of the fear that held us all in hostage. "We outnumber them."

"Wait," I said, fearing that any antagonistic gestures on our part would trigger the dogs and drive them into a murderous killing spree, putting us—or Alpert—in danger.

Strange words seemed to be coming out of Alpert's mouth—words of an unknown origin, if words they were. But the way he chanted them and assembled the bizarre syllables together told me he was attempting to say something. Perhaps he was trying to pray, but his lips and mouth were frozen, and he couldn't articulate properly. That's what I tried to convince myself of, though deep inside of me, I knew it was something else. It wasn't a prayer, nor a song any man had ever known. And recollections of the terrible and throaty dialect came back into my memory, for I had heard them a few times from Land himself—during stormy evenings at his London apartment, when he drank the awful piss he dared call rum as he recited passages from his infamously odious book of arcane knowledge. I wanted to clasp my hands over my ears. I wanted Alpert's voice to stop and this terrible sensation of dread that now invaded my very soul to die.

"He doesn't want us here!" cried Alpert, stammering. He stared again at me, fully and consciously, as if he could see. He pointed an accusing finger at me and went on. "We should have stayed away from his land. Now we are doomed. We all are, because of you."

"Who?" I asked, startled. "Who are you talking about?"

All the warmth vacated my body the moment Alpert's lips parted to pronounce the words: "The Unnamed One: The Elder God!"

A sudden gust of wind lifted a veil of snow, which momentarily obscured from our vision everything around us—the mountain ridge, the lead-coloured clouds, the mad dogs, and Alpert. Something even more hideous was dissimulated behind the sheet of insidious crystals. A shadow, unmistakably present. Feral and powerful.

Plaintive voices attacked my ears, superimposed over a series of guttural sound so horrible that I screamed at the top of my voice, trying to bury the demonic whistling of the wind and the terrible curse it seemed to be carrying with. The cacophony in my head turned into a debilitating pressure before it released suddenly. I raised my eyes back toward the snowy veil, which tumbled down quickly, revealing a horrendous hecatomb of severed bodies and blood-stained snow.

I fell to my knees and buried my head in my hands.

"Dear God, have mercy!"

CHAPTER IV

January 04, 1936

We have buried the severed bodies of the dogs as well as what remained of Alpert— whose head went missing. His body was torn so gruesomely that I am certain no pain as great as it was could have caused the poor fellow to contort in such a manner. We have given him, as well as the rest of Alpert's party, who I fear we will never find, a decent funeral and prayers, and we've gone on as best we could with our tasks despite the grief and the terror and torment assailing us all. We have plenty of work ahead of us before we can leave this satanic place and come back home. More importantly, we need to connect with Thomas and the rest of his crew. They haven't answered my calls yet. I pray to God that he is still alive...

I can't believe what happened, what we all saw. I can't believe the words I am scrawling on the yellowed pages of this diary—this truth that has led me to abort the mission. I will be called crazy and a madman upon return, and the words of my story vulgar phantasmagorical elucubrations. But in no way will I force any more of these poor souls to endure this orgy of madness. This continent has bestowed enough of its brutal evil on us. That thing—that shadow hidden behind the veil of snow, and the voices that haunted my soul, I can't forget them, and I fear I will never be able to. I am constantly seeing Alpert in my head, the deep, black sockets staring at me, and hearing the words he pronounced... I can't help but link them with the incantations Land's mouth often ejaculated, those concerning what I now know is called the Unnamed One, this Elder God.

It comes to me just now, as I recall the binge-drinking at Land's apartment and those thick, worn-out pages of the book Land turned so feverishly... His true motivation behind his voyage may have been utterly opposite to what he was approached for—which was to gather geological data and study the different strata of ice and the aeons-old sedimentary rock in a scientific effort to date the continent. No, I believe that Land had other interests in this expedition. I think he purposely sought out this "Unnamed One." I couldn't guess as to what drove him to suspect there was evidence of its presence here in this wasteland of cold, immaculate snow. I should have listened more closely to Land's stories. I should have, but I didn't.

"This is Thomas Lashly. Do you copy?" The voice from the radio startled me. I raised my head from the table on which I had fallen asleep and, wiping my mouth, answered Thomas excitedly.

"This is Captain Henry Chapelton. I copy. Thomas, come back to the camp right now. I repeat. Come back to the camp right now."

A short silence followed my transmission, filled with strange crackling and humming sounds, before I heard Thomas's voice again.

"We can't!" he shouted, his voice distorted and barely audible, like he was speaking too close to the microphone. It took a moment before he resumed, but nothing of what he said was decipherable except for these words: "…found a strange aperture and a cavern…foot of Mount Terror…Land's dead…Evidence of…"

And then nothing. The transmission cut out suddenly, leaving nothing but hissing and crackling static.

"Thomas, for God's sake, come back here right now! Alpert is dead. We are aborting the mission. We need to leave now. I beg you, Thomas, stop everything you are doing and come back here immediately. There is something going on here. Thomas…Thomas, do you hear me?"

The radio remained eerily silent for a long moment during which I remained still, too afraid, too disgusted by the resurgence of the strange guttural voices and bizarre language to move.

"Thomas!" I screamed through the microphone, expecting an answer or a call for help. I was ready for anything except what he said next, in a strange, throaty voice: "Leave."

"Thomas is at Mount Terror. We gotta go get him!" I yelled as I ran out of the tent, my coat unbuttoned and the cold slipping its icy fingers around my body and throat. "Thomas is…"

I halted in the middle of the camp, facing the desolation all around me. Vestiges of our expedition lay everywhere. The tents were tipped over, torn and dismantled like a horde of rabid creatures had just had their way with them. Oil and gasoline canisters, as well as boxes and other goods, were scattered throughout the area, partly hidden under a fine layer of fresh snow. But as for the men, there was no sign of them. I was all alone.

"Comanche? Robert? Can anyone hear me?" My voice travelled uninterrupted across an ethereal world of solitude. "Where are you? Where in the hell *are* you?"

A low, powerful growl roared under my feet, making the ground shake momentarily. Everywhere I looked, all I could see was darkness ascending slowly from some unknown origin. The *shadow* was there, everywhere. A bizarre smell filled the air, prominent and acrid like sulphur, making me dizzy. The rumbling resumed and grew unchecked, interspersed with the regular thumping of tambours beating the rhythm of some impossible Wagnerian symphony. And once again came the odious language, vomited out of the bowels of the earth, much louder than before.

"Stop!" I fell to my knees, my breathing becoming erratic. "Make it stop."

The sound of a single gunshot crossed ominously through the sky, putting an abrupt end to my crazy train of thought.

Thomas.

I started to run toward the shadowy rim of Mount Terror, ignoring the murderous shadow at my back. Whatever happened here, whatever the lurking danger, whatever was going to happen, I had to get to Thomas and help him. I had to take anyone who remained alive back to New Zealand—anywhere, as long as it was far from this forbidden land.

"Thomas!" The snow crust was thick and sharp and cut my skin through my pants, hurting me in a way I couldn't have imagined possible. Crossing a sea of spiky glass shards wouldn't have been this painful. I fired my revolver once, hoping he would respond. To my great relief, he did. "Hold on, I'm coming!"

I couldn't tell how much time had passed since I left the camp—or what was left of it. I didn't look over my shoulder until a strong gust of wind pushed against my back, as if guiding me in a particular direction. Nothing could have prepared me to witness what I did.

Covering the world behind me was the same shadow, now impossibly large. It appeared to have stretched out so much that my eyes couldn't find its beginning or its end. It seemed to move warily towards me, turning the pale-grey sky a dark purple and spreading an eternal darkness over the land.

Leave. Leave. Leave. I heard unhuman voices say, though if they were real or not, I couldn't tell. The guttural alien chanting resumed intermittently in a language so odd, I couldn't find the right syllables with which to transcribe it. In between episodes of chanting were great seismic tremors, as if they were connected somehow.

"I'm leaving. I'm leaving!" I yelled desperately, the words leaving my mouth without me being aware of them. It was like my body wanted to act of its own accord, my mouth wished to respond to the warning accordingly, and my legs desired to drive me towards the waters where the *Ulysses*'s hull lay. But not my head. I wanted to retrieve Thomas. I wanted him alive and with me. Whether or not navigating the insidious seas with so ridiculously small a crew was sheer madness, never would we perish in this unwelcoming land.

Thomas, I repeated in my head over and over again, trying to ignore the exhortation to leave, the abominable alien chant, and my growing repulsion towards Mount Terror—which seemed to be the ultimate origin of this madness. The storm had, after all, ended at its peak when we arrived. And this was where Thomas was.

"I'm coming."

CHAPTER V

January ?

Defying those ancient, cosmic laws was utter madness...I realise it now. Confronting them was just as suicidal. I shouldn't have. I shouldn't have. The chant echoes in my head more prominently now that I am rounding the foot of Mount Terror, and I know it has something to do with the partly buried peaks James Clark Ross so innocently yet perfectly baptised so many years ago, for terror was all it inspired. Terror, and nothing else.

If anyone finds this journal, please listen to me. LEAVE this place right away.

"Thomas! Thomas, where are you?" I shot once and then twice with my revolver, but the noise died almost instantly, just like the sound of my voice. Behind me, the great shadow was pushing me towards the ship, the outline of which was now visible over the icy bumps and mounds along the shore that the wind had moulded so grossly over the ages. The masts of the *Ulysses* swung and swayed like a vulgar toy boat in a churning sea of malice and trickery.

I resisted the constant pull towards the ship. I resisted *leaving,* but instead followed the chants—

followed Thomas. I resisted as strongly as I could. I cursed this land. Cursed all that I could curse. The purple sky. The storm. The wind. The snow. I cursed every single thing we had encountered since entering the Austral Sea. And moreover, I cursed myself for having led everyone here and not turning around when we should have.

And what faced me now shook me so deeply and shattered me so much that I considered pressing the barrel of my revolver against my temple and pulling the trigger, just to end it all. The only thing hindering me from doing so was the peculiar impression that here, in this damn land, even death might die. And never would I allow my soul to be trapped in such a purgatory for eternity.

The shadow, as horrible as it had appeared to me earlier, now surrounded me and covered the water nearby like an extension of unearthly darkness, blacker than anything I had ever seen.

Crooked strands of dark matter oozed from the murky waters, rising like mighty tentacles and restlessly pounding all around the *Ulysses*. Slowly, the monstrous shape took form before me, this shadow that could only be one entity, an extension of this land, of these seas.

The Unnamed One. The Elder God.

I stared helplessly while the mighty Octopoda—if overgrown mollusc of any kind it was—lifted the ship sky-high and pounded it against the icy waters, breaking it into hundreds of pieces and annihilating our last chance of escape. I stood in horror while the shadow—the *thing*—brought its tentacles out of the water again, a rampant abomination that crawled over the shoreline.

I searched the pockets of my coat and found a handful of cartridges, which I then loaded into my revolver. I emptied the barrel into this warped entity that was now surrounding me from all sides at once. I felt the tentacles approaching me like a mass of ardent embers. Burning spread along my left leg, and I dropped my head, noticing that the shadow was attempting to envelop me. I yelled and moved away from the thing, and for the first time, the *thing* scream back at me.

I ran towards the last remaining piece of land not claimed by the shadow. My body agreed that I had to flee from this evil scourge, even if there wasn't any chance of surviving. My feet urged me along the edge of strange crevices, some of which were easily six feet deep, and all of which converged towards the mouth of a cavern. I jumped down the nearest crevice and slipped down into a great vaulted room, where I hoped the *thing* wouldn't be able to reach me.

A green phosphorescence dimly illuminated the cavern, produced by strange fungi that ran all over the walls and the ceiling—something one shouldn't be able to find in such a remote and uninhabitable and cold place. I jogged away from the entry and fell over a pile of bags and apparatuses that were lying carelessly on the floor, as if they had been abandoned. I squatted and inspected the pile more carefully, recognising some of it as equipment from our expedition. Some of the other items seemed older. Under one of the bags was the same portable wireless transmitter I had given Thomas before he left. All appeared to be in working order.

"Thomas?" I yelled. "Thomas, where are you? Can anybody hear me?"

I waited anxiously for someone to answer, holding my breath and ignoring the thumping of my heart in my ears. But I received no response. Not even the barking of one of the dogs. The infamous chant has ceased, and now that I thought of it, from the moment the *thing* erupted from the water and destroyed the *Ulysses*, I seemed to be all alone. Thomas had disappeared, just like the crew back at camp. It didn't make sense at all. I'd heard gunshots. I'd heard Thomas calling over the radio. And the radio was right fucking there. *He should be here; he must be here.*

I walked around the cavern, ignoring for a moment the lurking danger outside. I searched for any doors or adjacent chambers, calling out Thomas's name and the names of the others in his party. After a moment of fumbling around, I finally reached the opening of a long, narrow tunnel that descended through the unfathomable abyss of Mount Terror. I placed my hands on both sides of the opening for support and pushed my head through the aperture, through which emanated a steady breeze of decay and rot.

"Thomas, are you down there?" I shouted. It took a moment before the echoes of my voice finally died out.

"Henry! Henry!" came Thomas's voice from the bottomless depth. It sounded strained and broken, interspersed with harsh sobs, as if he were suffering immeasurable pain and terror.

"Thomas! Are you all right?"

"Turn around, Henry!" he yelled back. "Turn around and leave this place. I beg you, do not come down here. It's too horrible. Land and the crew and the dogs…"

"Don't be a fool, Thomas. I'm coming. Hold on," I said, ignoring his warning and the bizarre sensation that assailed me upon hearing about Land and the crew. I placed a foot on the first slimy step of the stone-carved staircase. I held one hand against the wall to my right and had just started my descent when I felt some strange recesses and bumps under my fingers, too detailed and precise to have been formed naturally. I stopped and leaned in closer to a spot that was illuminated by a wide patch of the glowing fungi.

Symbols and pictographs covered the wall, resembling something I was certain I had seen before but was unable to recall precisely. Though simple and, to some extent, primitive, what they represented sufficed to fill me with a dread greater than the thought of death itself. There it was, right before me, the titanic shadow whose shape shrouded the whole continent as if *it* was the continent, and Mount Terror was at its very centre, its heart. Dozens of gigantic tentacles extended menacingly across the sea as far as the shores of nearby continents, and its eyes and its mouth… Dear God, I couldn't even describe them. It was all too horrible, too abominable. I let the shiver pass as I moved on from the engraving, which I now realised was a depiction of the Unnamed One—the Elder God. The next was a group of about twenty or twenty-five strange, eyeless creatures, slender in shape, kneeling before the great *thing*. Some of them held round objects I would describe as tambours.

Just as I began to make the connection between these strange engravings and past events, Thomas resumed his whining, beseeching me to not come to his rescue. He screamed, and his voice rose into an indecipherable shriek, his words becoming less and less coherent until he burst out laughing maniacally. The alien chant began again, and the tambours resumed their ghastly ceremony.

"It's over, Henry. It's over. They're coming."

The chant and the noise of the tambours grew in intensity as if coming closer to me, sending tremors across the ground under my feet. This was followed by hot bursts of gaseous sulphur that seized my lungs and made me cough harshly. They were coming my way—the eyeless, slender creatures, the worshipers of the Elder God.

I climbed up the few steps I had descended and ran across the vaulted room, unable to escape the debilitating chant and the steady and powerful *po-pom* of the tambours, which was causing the walls to tremble despite that they were made of solid stone. Everywhere I looked, all I could see now was the ancient engraving, which I now remembered seeing in Land's book. Outside the cavern the wind howled furiously, blowing and screaming in some twisted harmony with the growling of the *thing*.

I stopped by Thomas's wireless transmitter and hastily turned it on, hoping the batteries weren't already dead. The pilot light turned red, and I adjusted the frequency, all too aware that there was no way the signal would go anywhere past the antenna at our camp—if there still was one. I nonetheless picked up the microphone and placed it near my lips, fantasising that the radio frequencies would travel across the Austral Sea to be caught back in New Zealand. The eyeless creatures were close, the noise of their tambours deafening and their chant oppressive.

"This is Captain Henry Chapelton!" I screamed into the microphone. "The *Ulysses* has sunk. I repeat—the *Ulysses* has sunk. Everyone's dead. Do not come to rescue us. I repeat—do not come and rescue us. For God's sake, never send anyone here again…"

ABOUT THE AUTHOR

E.L. GILES writes horror and science-fiction, from the weirdest of the cosmic tales to the most brutal and unsettling kind of dystopian story one can think of. He has authored and self-published two novels and one novelette and is currently finishing his third novel. Death, solitude, desperation, helplessness, weakness, and human nature are some of the main themes his stories generally gravitate around. Rarely do his stories divert from being extremely dark, with a thick ambiance and full of vivid descriptions

Giles doesn't give in to the fast-paced, action-packed stories, but the ones that set you into a unique and intense mood.

Bibliography

ANGELS, Black Hare Press, 2019

APOCALYPSE, Black Hare Press, 2019

BEYOND, Black Hare Press, 2019

Deep Space, Black Hare Press, 2019

IT COMES FROM THE SKY, Eerie Rivers, 2020

LOCKDOWN horror 2, Black Hare Press, 2020

LOCKDOWN horror 4, Black Hare press, 2020

LOCKDOWN sci-fi 2, Black Hare Press, 2020

MONSTERS, Black Hare Press, 2019

OCEANS, Black Hare Press, 2020

QUIETUS, Black Hare Press, 2020

THE BERRYMAN HOUSE, 2019

THE BIRDMAN PROJECT Book 1, 2019

THE BIRDMAN PROJECT Book 2, 2019

UNRAVEL, Black Hare Press, 2019

WORLDS, Black Hare Press, 2019

Connect

Website: www.elgilesauthor.com

Amazon: amazon.com/author/elgiles

Facebook: @elgilesauthor

ABOUT THE PUBLISHER

BLACK HARE PRESS is a small, independent publisher based in Melbourne, Australia.

Founded in 2018, our aim has always been to champion emerging authors from all around the globe and offer opportunities for them to participate in speculative fiction and horror short story anthologies.

Connect

Website: *www.blackharepress.com*

Twitter: *@BlackHarePress*